Every Blessing!

F.M. Strand

ISBN 978-1-60131-008-8

© 2007 Scott Stroud
Illustrations © 2007 Jim Hunt

Scott & Mary Stroud
6066 Shingle Creek Parkway
PMB #186
Brooklyn Center, MN 55430
US United States
612-850-8511

For more information about Home's Cool,
visit www.homescoolkids.com

Printed in the United States of America

Published with the assistance of Big Tent Books.

Dedicated to our veterans.
Thank you for all that you sacrificed
in service of our country!
May the next generation learn to give you
the honor that you deserve.

The first time he saw Mr. Grady, Peter was helping his dad move the last of the big boxes into their new house. One thing was certain…

Mr. Grady didn't seem happy to see them.

Dad noticed Mr. Grady as well. He walked right over to the fence and stuck out his hand for Mr. Grady to shake. Mr. Grady just looked at him with a sour expression while his bulldog growled a greeting from behind him.

"I see you have kids," he sneered, like kids were some kind of disease.

"I have four of them!" Dad beamed, his hand still hanging in the air.

"Well, tell them to stay off of my grass and keep quiet! I like my peace," stated Mr. Grady.

"My children won't be a bother to you," said Dad. "I'll make sure they stay out of your yard."

"General Patton will make sure of it too," said Mr. Grady, patting his dog's wide head.

With that, the old man and his dog turned and marched into their house.

The next time Peter saw Mr. Grady, he and his brother, Elijah, were helping a new friend down the street rake her leaves. Mr. Grady and General Patton were out for a walk.

"Shouldn't you kids be in school?" he snorted, when he saw them.

"We're home schooled, sir, and sometimes our mom has us help others as part of our lessons," said Peter.

"Home schooled? I guess that means you'll be around all the time!" said Mr. Grady as he stared at them suspiciously. "Forward march, General!" he commanded as they turned on their heels and continued down the sidewalk.

The next day the boys were playing football out in the back yard and Peter was trying out his long bomb.

"Go deep, Elijah!" he yelled as he fired off a high one.

The football soared up into the sky, over Elijah's head and right into Mr. Grady's vegetable patch.

The back door of Mr. Grady's house flew open. General Patton stormed over and scooped up the ball into his drooling mouth. He gave the boys a snort and back inside he went as a smiling Mr. Grady held the door for him.

"Oh no!" said Elijah. "Now our ball is a chew toy."

As the days got colder, they saw less of Mr. Grady, and when they did see him, he was walking with a limp.

"I think Mr. Grady has a bad leg," said Mom.
"Maybe that's why he's not very friendly."

The first morning of December started out dark and cloudy. While they did school work, Peter and Elijah listened to the news reporter saying that a record-setting blizzard was on its way. By lunch time, the snow was piled up to the first step.

By bedtime, the snow was past Dad's knees and, by the time it stopped the next morning, the door was blocked shut. Dad and the boys had to climb out the window in order to start shoveling.

While they were working, they noticed some movement coming from Mr. Grady's place. He was trying to push the front door open but it wouldn't budge.

"Come on, boys," said Dad. "We have a trapped neighbor."

"But Dad, he told us to never go near his house!" said Peter worriedly.

"I know, son, but sometimes God wants you to reach out your hand even though it might get bit."

They worked hard for about an hour before they finally reached Mr. Grady's front door. As soon as they broke through the snow pile, the door burst open and a very uncomfortable looking General Patton came barreling out.

Mr. Grady's head slowly poked out and he smiled. "I thought the General was going to have a major accident. He has been waiting to get out and use the fire hydrant all morning!"

A relieved General Patton came bounding around the snow bank and started licking Peter's hand.

"Umm...would you men like to come in for a mug of hot cocoa?" asked Mr. Grady.

"That would be great," said Dad. "It's cold out here!"

Mr. Grady looked at Peter and said, "Besides, I have something that belongs to you, young man."

After Mr. Grady had served them their hot cocoa, he led Peter into his office. As Peter entered, his eyes bugged out! He had never seen so many war medals and awards in his whole life!

"Are you a hero?" Peter asked in amazement.

Mr. Grady held up a special looking purple medal to show Peter. "I earned this one by not being able to outrun a bullet," he said with a wink. "The bullet is right here in my leg."

"Really?" said Peter.

Mr. Grady had just become the bravest man he had ever met.

Mr. Grady reached up on a shelf and pulled down Peter's football and handed it to him.

"The General only chewed it up a little bit."

"Thank you, sir," said Peter.

"Maybe next week you could come visit me and I can give you a homeschool lesson about the big War," said Mr. Grady.

"I would love that!" exclaimed Peter.

Mr. Grady stood up as straight as his old body would allow him, saluted Peter and said, "Dismissed, soldier!"

They both returned to the living room where Dad was sipping his hot cocoa and Elijah was playing with General Patton. Mr. Grady walked over and placed a hand on Dad's shoulder.

"You know, I guess home-schooled kids aren't so bad after all," he said with a chuckle.

Dad smiled. He had to agree.

The End

"You shall rise before the gray headed
and honor the presence of an old man,
and fear your God: I *am* the LORD."

Leviticus 19:32 NKJ

Author's note:

Having been a barber for over 15 years now, I have
had the privilege of hearing numerous stories from
the gray haired men that have sat in my chair week
after week. I have learned much about interesting
people, exotic places and a simpler time in the history
of our nation. My hope is that this book will inspire
our children to take the first steps in reaching out to
the honored veterans among us, because they have so
much to share.

— Scott Stroud

About the Author and Illustrator

Scott and his wife, Mary, are the founders of Stroud Family Ministries. In April of 2007 they will begin traveling the country in a motor home with their four children. They will be bringing their Home's Cool Kids books to conventions from Rhode Island to Oregon and encouraging families wherever they are. To contact them, go to www.HomesCoolKids.com.

Jim Hunt is a graduate of the Massachusetts College of Art in Boston and has been illustrating professionally since 1989. Aside from illustrating books, Jim's art has been in dozens of magazines, and his political cartoons run nationally.

Jim lives with his wife and two daughters along the Chesapeake Bay in Annapolis, MD. He can be contacted through www.BigTentBooks.com.